Read with Mummy

Cinderella

Story retold by Janet Brown
Illustrations by Ken Morton

D1135633

Once upon a time a rich baron and his lovely daughter lived in a castle. They rode horses and read books and had many adventures together.

The baron's wife had died many years before, but he wanted his daughter to have a new mother. So one day he married a beautiful widow who had two daughters of her own.

What kind of things did the baron and his daughter
like doing together?

Shortly afterwards the baron died, leaving his little girl in the care of her stepmother.

Now, the stepmother was not wicked but, as the years passed, she grew sad and bitter. She spent all her time with her own girls and ignored the baron's daughter. Soon the baron's daughter was little more than a servant in the castle. She washed the dishes, made all the clothes and slept in the kitchen among the cinders.

And so she became known as Cinderella.

Why do you think the baron's daughter became known as "Cinderella"?

One day an invitation arrived from the palace.
"It's the prince's birthday!" said the older stepsister,
who was very vain.

"He's going to choose a bride!" said the younger
stepsister, who was rather silly.

"This is your big chance, my pets!" said their mother.
"Cinderella will make your ballgowns and soon we
shall be living like queens in the palace!"

Why do you think Cinderella's stepsisters were so excited about the prince's birthday ball?

Cinderella worked hard making dresses for her stepsisters. She had no time to make herself a dress. When the day of the ball came, her stepsisters laughed at her and her stepmother said coldly: "Poor Cinderella! You simply can't come to the palace in old clothes."

Whilst every young lady in the land danced at the prince's birthday ball, Cinderella sat alone by the fire in her rags.

Why wasn't Cinderella allowed to go to the ball?

Suddenly there was a tap on the door and Cinderella's fairy godmother flew in!

"We haven't much time to get you to the ball!" she cried. "Now, stand back!"

She waved her wand and everything around them was transformed. The pumpkin became a carriage, the mice became footmen, and Cinderella's rags became a ballgown of gold and pearls.

"My magic only lasts until midnight," warned the fairy godmother. "Now, go and have a wonderful time, my dear!"

How long does the fairy godmother's magic last?

In the palace everything went quiet as a beautiful stranger entered the ballroom. The prince, who had been feeling bored and unhappy, looked up and saw the girl of his dreams. He asked her to dance and then he danced with her all night. Soon he knew that he had found his bride.

Cinderella's stepmother and stepsisters were furious – but they didn't recognise the stranger!

Do you know who the beautiful stranger was that danced
with the prince all night?

Cinderella was so happy that she forgot her fairy godmother's warning until the clocks struck midnight! Then she ran out of the prince's arms into the night. As she ran, her dress turned to rags and her footmen turned to mice.

"Stop!" cried the prince. "Where will I find you again?"

He chased after her but all he found was her small glass slipper.

What happened to Cinderella's footmen at midnight?
(Clue: look at the picture!)

"I will marry whoever fits this slipper," said the prince. He sent his courtiers to search the length and the breadth of the land. Finally they arrived at the baron's castle.

With great excitement Cinderella's stepsisters tried on the slipper but, like everyone else, their feet were too big.

"Try harder!" cried their mother, and she even tried it on herself!

When no one was looking, Cinderella slipped her foot into the slipper.

"We have found the prince's bride!" said the delighted courtiers.

Why did every woman in the land try on the small glass slipper?

Cinderella was carried to the palace in triumph. The heartbroken prince was overjoyed to see her, and they were married the very next day.

Cinderella's stepmother and stepsisters were sorry for their unkindness. Cinderella invited them to visit her at the palace and, in time, they all became friends and lived happily ever after.

Who ended up living in the palace after all?

On a piece of paper practise writing these words:

Cinderella asleep

pumpkin

mice

glass slipper

broom